MY LiFe as a Tarantula Toe Tickler

the incredible worlds of **Wally McDoogle**

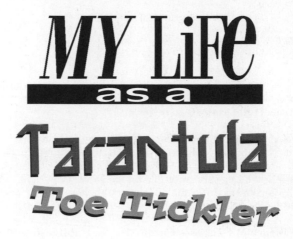

MY LiFe
as a
Tarantula
Toe Tickler

BILL MYERS

Tommy
NELSON

www.tommynelson.com

A Division of Thomas Nelson, Inc.
www.ThomasNelson.com

Published in Nashville, Tennessee, by Tommy Nelson®, a Division of Thomas Nelson, Inc. Visit us on the Web at www.tommynelson.com.

Verses marked (TLB) are from *The Living Bible*. Copyright © 1971. Used by permission of Tyndale House Publishers, Inc., Wheaton, Illinois 60189. All rights reserved.

Library of Congress Cataloging-in-Publication Data

Myers, Bill, 1953-
    My life as a tarantula toe tickler / Bill Myers.
        p. cm. -- (The incredible worlds of Wally McDoogle ; 22)
        Summary: Rather than facing the consequences of breaking his mother's incredibly expensive new vase, disaster-prone Wally McDoogle becomes involved with Junior Whiz Kid's zany experiments and must face a giant flying snail and a tarantula the size of a small house.
    ISBN 0-8499-5993-4 (pbk.)
    [1. Responsibility—Fiction. 2. Conduct of life--Fiction. 3. Humorous stories.]   I. Title. II. Series: Myers, Bill, 1953-   . Incredible worlds of Wally McDoogle ; 22.
PZ7.M98234Mylf 2003
[Fic]—dc22   2003004132

Printed in the United States of America

04 05 06 07 PHX 5

For Sue Holtsnider:
A role model of love and
commitment.

"Admit your faults to one another . . ."

—James 5:16 (TLB)

Contents

Chapter 1

Just for Starters ...

Look, I know it was wrong. I know I should have told my folks. But when a guy gets older, there are some things he likes to work out on his own.

"And some things he should never try!"

(Sorry, didn't mean to yell. I only yell when things get to me. So . . .)

"And some things he should never try!"

(If you guessed this one got to me, your guesser guessed the right guess.)

It all started innocently enough—which should have been my first clue something was wrong (at least in these stories). Mom had just bought this incredibly expensive vase and put it on this incredibly expensive vase stand.

"Now everyone be careful," she said. "This is an incredibly expensive vase, and I've just put it on this incredibly expensive vase stand."

(Told you.)

"Yes, Mother dearest," little sister Carrie sweetly answered. (An obvious clue she was heading to the mall and needed money.)

"Umph," my twin brothers, Burt and Brock, grunted in unison. (An obvious clue they were watching football on TV.)

"*Snork—wheeeeze* . . . ," Dad answered. (An obvious clue he was lying on the sofa examining the inside of his eyelids.)

Then there was my own answer, which I saved until she'd left the room:

"AUGH!"
K-Thud!

For you newbies, that's the sound I make when stepping on our cat, Collision (who did not get his name by accident). You see, he has this bad habit of sleeping at the top of the stairs, which is no problem, except I have an even worse habit of tripping over him—which led to the rest of my answer

k-bounce, k-bounce, k-bounce
sprain-a-wrist-here, bruise-a-face-there

as I tumbled down the steps, managing to break numerous body parts along the way.

Oh, and there were two other things I included in the answer for good measure. The first, was my world-famous

K-rash!

(which is the sound of an incredibly clumsy human slamming into an incredibly expensive vase stand).

And finally (don't pretend you didn't know this was coming), the ever-popular

*K-shatter
tinkle, tinkle, tinkle*

(which, of course, is the sound of an incredibly expensive vase shattering into a thousand incredibly little pieces).

Now it was time for quick, cool thinking . . . for calm, heroic action . . . for running around like a chicken with my head cut off (actually, *crawling* around like a chicken with my head cut off, since I'd just broken one or more legs).

The point is, I couldn't get blamed for breaking the vase! Why should I? It's not like it was *my* fault. I mean, who in their right mind would put something breakable within my reach? And so close to the stairs? Didn't Mom know I specialized in stairway disasters? (Everybody needs a hobby.) Wasn't she there when Dad built a padded wall at the bottom of the steps to cut down on our trips to the emergency room? . . . And who put the cat at the top of the stairs?

So, instead of admitting that I might be just the tiniest bit responsible, I did what any normal, guilty, afraid-to-get-in-trouble kid would do . . . I tried desperately to cover things up and not get caught!

First, I scampered across the floor, grabbing all the pieces I could find. Then I tried putting them back together by stacking them on top of each other. A great idea if I was trying to stack bricks for a wall—not so great if I was trying to stack pieces for a round and curvy vase.

Obviously, I needed a little glue. No problem. I dashed into the kitchen, yanked open the drawer, and found it. I should have suspected it might have been a little old when the label read:

WARNING. Use in well-ventilated caves.
Keep out of the reach of pet dinosaurs.

But I had more important things on my mind . . . like trying to open it.

Actually, that wasn't a problem. All I had to do was take the little straight pin and "OW!" poke it into "OW! OW!" the little "OW! OW! OW!" nozzle and *not* into "OW! OW! OW! OW!" my hand.

As soon as I got my wounds bandaged up and swung by the hospital for a blood transfusion, I returned to the kitchen, squeezed the tube, and out came:

spiff . . .

That's right. Not "*splat*," not "*splurt*," not even the ever-popular "*squirt.*" This tube was so old and dry that instead of glue, it just shot out a little cloud of dust.

Then I heard footsteps approaching the kitchen. I knew this was no time to panic. All I had to do was stay calm and go to Plan B. Except for one minor problem:

"THERE WAS NO PLAN B!"

(I'm shouting again. Sorry. I always get a little nervous when I'm about to die.)

The footsteps grew closer. Then came the voice. "Wally, *snap-snap, pop-pop,* whatcha doin'?"

I sighed in relief. The footsteps and voice belonged to my little sister Carrie. The *snap-snap, pop-pop* belonged to the two packs of gum she always chewed.

"Hey, squirt," I said as she entered. "What's up?"

"We're just, *snap-snap,* going to the, *pop-pop,* mall."

"We?"

Suddenly, a half-dozen of her fellow munchkins trotted in, all heading for the back door—*snapping* and *popping* away on their own gum. Oh, and *giggling,* lots of *giggling.* Why is it that little sisters are always giggling (I mean, when they're not busy tattling)?

And at the back of the crowd was one Megan Melkner. The poor thing had a major crush on me. (I know, go figure.) It was either my incredible good looks, my marvelous physique . . . or the fact that she desperately needed glasses. Then there was her voice. I don't want to be mean, but it sounded like fingernails on a blackboard in the middle of a pig-squealing contest (with plenty of microphone feedback).

"Hi, Wallace," she squeaked as she batted her eyes and flashed a grin so bright that I needed sunglasses to look at her.

"Hi," I mumbled, trying to stop my face from twitching. My face always twitched when I talked to her—just like it twitches when I see train wrecks on TV or murderers on the nightly news.

"Whatcha doin'?"

More eye batting. More grinning.

"I'm trying to glue something, but this stupid glue doesn't work."

"That's too bad." More batting, more grinning.

"Yeah." More twitching.

"Hey, why don't you try this?" Suddenly, she stuck out her tongue. On it sat a huge wad of Chewie Blewie bubblegum. "Hewre." (Which is as close as anyone can get to "here" with their tongue sticking out with a wad of gum sitting on it.)

"I'm sorry, what?"

"Ooze ma umm." (Translation: "Use my gum.")

"What??"

She pulled in her tongue just long enough to speak human-ese. "This gum is way stickier than any glue." Then she stuck it back out.

I stared at the glistening pink wad on her tongue, then gave the only answer I could think of:

"Eewww!"
(Translation: *"Eewww!"*)

"No, Wallace, I'm serious," she said, flashing

more teeth and batting more eyes. "I'd consider it such an honor if you would use my gum."

The other girls must have thought it was a cool idea, too, because they also surrounded me—each sticking out their tongue, each crying, "Mime, poo! Mime, poo! Ooze ma umm, poo!"

"Wally, what's going on down there?" Mom called from upstairs.

I froze. If she came down before I fixed the vase, I knew my goose was cooked, my milk spilled, my toast burned—(Hey, I'm in a kitchen; what type of comparisons do you expect me to dream up?)

Luckily, Carrie came to my rescue. "It's just some of my friends, Mom."

"Okay," she called, "but don't go spilling any milk or burning any toast."

I whispered to Carrie in astonishment, "How'd she know?"

"And no goose cooking!" Mom finished.

I looked to Carrie, who shrugged. "Got me," she said.

Meanwhile, Megan Melkner and the rest of her gang continued closing in and begging, "Ooze ma umm, poo! Ooze ma umm, poo!"

Time was running out. And since I could see no other choice, I reluctantly held out my hand to them and *k-spit, k-spit, k-spit*

suddenly, I was holding more gum than you find under a school cafeteria table.

And still they continued their selfless contributions:

k-spit, k-spit, k-spit
Haawk-spituwee!

"Hey, just gum!" I shouted.

"Sorry," a girl with bad allergies and no tissue muttered.

At last they finished and headed out the door for the mall. Not, of course, without Megan Melkner batting her eyes and flashing her smile one final time. "Good-bye, Wallace."

Poor kid, she was so hung up on me, and now she was obviously waiting for some caring, thoughtful reply. Unfortunately, the best I could come up with was, "Maybe you should seek professional help."

But it did the trick. She smiled dreamily and shuffled out the door with the rest of the herd for an evening at the mall.

At last I was alone holding a wad of gum the size of Mount Rushmore. I was also being exposed to more girl germs than the time I accidentally used Mom's toothbrush (and you thought the gum thing was gross). Anyway, I ran into the hallway, picked up the pieces of the vase, and started gluing (or gumming) them back together as fast as I could.

It was like a giant jigsaw puzzle. But gradually, piece by piece, it started coming together.

Somewhere in the back of my mind I knew I should tell Mom. I knew I should admit what had happened. But right now this gluing thing seemed a lot easier. And it was. Well, except the gum was still so warm and soft and juicy—(repeat after me . . . *Eewww!* Very good, class)—that the pieces wouldn't hold and kept collapsing.

No problem, I'd just hang around, uncollapsing them until the gum finally hardened and they stayed put. Of course, that looked like it would be sometime around 3:30 the next morning. But, I figured I could wait.

I'd just grab Ol' Betsy—my laptop computer—plop down in the hallway, and do some superhero writing. Oh, sure, it might be a little inconvenient, but anything was better than telling the truth and admitting my mistake. Unfortunately, that mistake was no mistake compared to the mistake I was mistakenly making when I mistakenly mistook this mistake as a minor mistake.

Confused?

Of course. But why should your life be any different from mine? (Unless, of course, you actually have one.)

Bottom line? Buckle up, ladies and gentlemen, boys and girls . . . 'cause we're about to hit some major McDoogle turbulence!

Chapter 2

Let the Failures Begin

I parked in the hallway with Ol' Betsy and started writing, glad to get my mind off the broken vase.

It's been a superlong day for our stupendously superswell and stunningly striking (not to mention staggeringly stupefying) superhero...

(Insert drum roll here.)

the incredibly intelligent...
the magnificently marvelous...
the outrageously original...

(What, you're still reading these intros and haven't skipped ahead?

Don't you have anything else better
to do?) Well, all right...
The one and only...(Here it comes.)
...the greatest of the great...(Are you
ready?)...The best of the best...(Are
you sure?)...Ladies and gentlemen,
it's...Burping Boy!

(Insert fanfare music and
wild applause!
No?
Okay, how 'bout polite clapping?
Ah, come on.
All right then, I'll settle for
quiet breathing and a heartbeat.
Thank you, thank you very much!)

Just hours earlier our middle-aged
hero had settled a dispute between
Diet Coke and Pepsi One over which
created the loudest burps. (Results
will be published in the upcoming
issue of *Belchweek* magazine.)
Then there was the Third Annual
Baby Burpathon at the baby formula
plant. (His baby came in second, but
only because the winner cheated by
eating a ton of green peppers first.)

And least, but not last, he picked up his older son, who was suspended from school for burping in answer to a teacher's question.

"But, Dad," Burping Jr. protested. "He was asking what I had for breakfast."

"What did you say?"

"BELCHem waffles."

Now, after a delightful (and somewhat noisy) dinner of radishes and ginger ale (yum), and a belchtime story for Baby Burp, our gaseous good guy is finally ready for bed when, suddenly,

Burpa-burpa!
Burpa-burpa!

(If you guessed that was the Burpa-phone ringing, you guessed correctly.)

Burpa-burpa!
Burpa-burpa!

(If you didn't, you haven't been reading enough of these stories.)

"Hello?" our hero answers.

"Burping Boy, is that you?"

"Hello??"

"Burping Boy?"

"Burping Boy! You've got the phone upside down again!"

"I can't hear you; I've got the phone upside down."

"Then turn it around!"

"What?"

"Turn it—"

"Hang on just a second, let me turn it around." In a flash of genius, our hero turns the phone around and hears the President of the United States shouting:

"Burping Boy, we need your help!"

"Someone's serving flat 7 UP again?"

"It's worse than that!"

"I'm sorry, Mr. President, nothing's worse than flat 7 UP."

"Yes!" cries the voice. "Giant dust bunnies—*crackle-crackle*—taking over—*hiss-hiss*—"

"Mr. President. You're breaking up. Please repeat!"

"I said, giant—*crackle-crackle*—

are—*hiss—hiss*—the world and you're the only one who can—*crackle-hiss, hiss-crackle*—"

"Mr. President! Mr. President, can you hear me?!"

But it does no good. All he hears is the *crackle-crackle* of the static, the *hiss-hiss* of a line going bad, and the—

giggle-giggle
chomp-chomp

Wait a minute! What was that?

giggle-giggle

It sounds like it's coming from under the bed.

chomp-chomp

What on earth?

Suddenly, our superhero drops his superhead to spy under his superbed. And, sure enough, there is someone or something underneath. Someone or something that is *giggle-giggling* while it is busy *chomp-chomping* through our superhero's phone line.

But this is not your everyday someone or something. You know better than that. No way, this is a giant dust bunny that's *giggle-giggling* and *chomp-chomping*.

Oh, and it's doing one other thing...

It's growing at least a foot high with every giggle it's giggling and chomp it's chomping!

Suddenly, the mattress begins bulging from underneath.

"Hey!"

And still the dust bunny continues giggling and chomping and growing.

Now, the mattress begins to tear.

"Hey! Hey!"

And still the creature continues with the *giggling* and *chomping*... until its head finally pops through and—

"Wally, what are you doing up this time of night?"

I looked up from my computer to see one

very sleepy Mom standing at the top of the stairs. "I know you love writing, but it's late. Go to bed."

I threw a panicked look toward the vase. The gum finally seemed to be holding. But you could still see the little cracks. I knew she'd eventually find out, but not right away. She was always so busy running around doing the mom things that I figured I'd have a week or two before she slowed down enough to notice. That gave me three options.

1. Tell her the truth and take responsibility for what I'd done.
2. Buy another vase and replace it without telling her. (But since the vase was expensive and I'd need a ton of money to replace it, that led me to the scariest option of all . . .)
3. Ask Wall Street, my best friend—even if she is a girl—for help.

Unfortunately, since number three was the worst choice, it was the only choice I could make.

* * * * *

"No problem," Wall Street said as we strolled down the street early the next morning. Actually, she strolled; I sort of sleepwalked. (Getting only forty-five minutes of sleep the night before will do that to a guy.) But that didn't slow her down. No sir, when it comes to making money, nothing slows down Wall Street.

"I've got thousands of ideas that'll make us both rich," she said.

I should have been suspicious. Not because she had thousands of ideas, but because she used the word "us"—as in making "*us* both rich." You see, Wall Street plans to make her first million by the time she's fourteen. And, so far, she's been making most of it off me.

Unfortunately, not only was I sleepwalking, but I was also sleepthinking, which would explain the rest of our conversation.

"So, what do you think?"

"That'zzz nizzzzz. . . ."

"Wally, wake up."

"Huh . . . ?"

"So do we have a deal?"

"What's that?"

"I think up the ideas, and you pay me a pile of money to use them. Do we have a deal?"

"That'zzz nizzzzz. . . ."

The next time I woke up, I was five dollars poorer and the proud owner of a brand-new business. I don't remember the details, but the ad in the newspaper read:

WALLY'S RECYCLED DENTAL FLOSS
Want to do your part in keeping the earth green? Then buy Wally's preowned dental floss! Taken from the garbage of people with only the least diseased gums, the floss is not only softer from its previous use, but slimier, too, allowing you to slip it in between those hard-to-floss places!

A foolproof plan, right? I mean, who wouldn't want to reuse someone else's dental floss? And look how it would be helping the environment. Unfortunately, it involved me having to climb into people's garbage cans late at night to search and retrieve the stuff. Even that wasn't so bad except for my allergy to watchdogs. I kept breaking out into a bad case of dog bites every time they attacked me.

So, we scrapped that idea, and I purchased the next ad . . .

WALLY'S BOTTLED CAR EXHAUST
Hey, those of you from the big cities. Tired of getting homesick whenever you go on vacations

**or weekend getaways? Then all you need to do
is buy a jar of Wally's Bottled Exhaust. As soon
as those homesick feelings start acting up, just
unscrew the lid, take a few whiffs, and it's like
you've never left home. Good for the entire family. You'll never have to go without pollution
again.**

Another brilliant idea, except for the part
about me having to sneak up to cars at stop-
lights to collect the fumes. No problem, except
all those tread marks can do a number on your
clothes . . . not to mention your body.

But that didn't slow us down. No sir. Not as
long as Wall Street had ideas and I was foolish
enough to buy them.

Next up . . .

CELEBRITY DANDRUFF

**Imagine impressing that certain someone with
flakes from the head of his or her favorite
celebrity. Just think of having that flaky powder
in a jar on the mantel. Better yet, buy the giant
econo-size and sprinkle it on your own shoul-
ders to give yourself that same star attraction.**

Not bad, except we didn't know any celebrities with dandruff. Come to think of it, we didn't

know any celebrities without dandruff. Other than that, it was a foolproof plan.

By now I was getting tired in an exhausted kind of way. But still, we continued. "What else you got?" I asked.

Wall Street frowned. "I just talked to Junior Whiz Kid on my cell phone."

"Junior Whiz Kid?" I asked. "The seven-year-old brainiac?"

"That's the one. He says he needs a lab assistant, so I thought of you."

"No way!" I cried.

"Why not? He'll pay good money and—"

"His inventions are nuts! Whacko! Insane!"

"And your point is . . . ?"

"What else have you got?"

"I've only got a couple more ideas, Wally. That's why I thought working for Junior might—"

"Let's try them!" I said.

"But—"

"Anything but Junior!"

"Anything?" she asked.

"Anything!"

"Well, all right. . . ."

Which, of course, led us to:

BAD BREATH SPRAY
Like going out on dates but hate those icky,

gross kisses? Well, fret no more. Just two squirts of Wally's Awful Bad Breath Spray and no one will ever want to kiss you again. Guaranteed to last for hours and to give you the reputation you want and deserve.

Another brilliant plan, except the only breath we could find that was bad enough belonged to my brother Burt (or was it his twin, Brock? I can never keep them straight). No problem. It just meant sneaking up on him when he was asleep and capturing his morning breath in a jar. Again, no problem, except the part where he kept catching me and rearranging my facial parts. Then there was his breath. I don't want to say it was bad, but every container we tried melted on contact with the fumes.

"Mommfs meext?" I asked. It was supposed to be "What's next?" but that's the best I could do with my face stitched and bandaged from Brock's (or was it Burt's?) morning greeting.

"Well, there's still Junior's offer," Wall Street answered.

"MO MWAY!"

"All right, all right, don't blow your stitches about it. I do have one other idea."

"MOKAY!" I shouted.

"It might be a little dangerous, and it might cost you a little extra, but—"

"MOKAY! MOKAY! MET'S MOO IT! MET'S MOO IT!"

"All right," she sighed. "But just remember, I warned you."

Chapter 3

Junior to the Rescue!

Wall Street stood at the foot of the stairs and thrust a newspaper ad into my hands. One look at it told me I was in trouble. Big trouble.

BECOME A WALKING DISASTER AREA
Tired of being athletic and coordinated?
Frustrated at never getting to wear full-body
casts? Then learn the secret art of clumsiness
from the world's all-time pro—the #1 Master of
Disaster . . . Mr. Wally McDoogle!

I finished reading the ad, then lowered it and gave Wall Street my world-famous death glare.

"Hey, it's either that or we call Junior Whiz Kid," she said.

"But this is crazy," I argued.

"It's a natural," she said. "People do take classes from experts."

"But who in their right—or wrong—mind would want to try to be like me?!"

"You're famous," she argued. "You're a household name. When people think 'klutz,' they think Wally McDoogle."

"Yeah, but—"

"They think broken bones and body parts, they think you."

"Yeah, but—"

"Mad dashes to the hospital for multiple organ transplants, you're the man."

"Yeah, but—"

Wall Street looked at me, waiting for more. But, as you can tell, I'd about run out of all my good arguments. Of course, I could fall back on the tried-and-true 'I know you are, but what am I,' but somehow it didn't quite fit.

"Besides," Wall Street finished, "your first customer is already waiting outside on the porch."

Before I could protest, or suggest the person get a brain implant, the door opened and in walked, *snap-snap, giggle-giggle,* you guessed it, Megan Melkner.

"Hello, Wallace," she said, batting her baby blues.

"Megan?" I felt my face twitch. "What are you doing here?"

"Why, learning to be just like you, of course."
More eye batting and gum snapping. Oh, and
let's not forget the grinning—lots and lots of
grinning.

I'll save you the boring details (along with
the additional face twitchings) and just get to
the headlines. As a klutz, she wasn't half bad,
at least for an amateur. And when I told her so,
she sighed dreamily and said, "I guess it comes
from all those months of watching you."

(Insert more face twitching here.)

We covered most of the basics. First, of
course, there was the standard

K-thud, K-thud, K-thud

stair falling.

"Not bad," I said, helping her to her feet.

"Thank you," she whispered, batting her
eyes romantically.

My face twitched faster.

Next came the basic tripping over one's
shadow, then being run over in traffic. She was
a great student, but all the eye batting, gum
snapping, and tooth glaring (not to mention face
twitching) was making me more than a little
crazy.

As we ended the lesson for the day and I

closed the door behind Megan, I heard Wall Street say, "Well, now, that went rather nicely."

To which I calmly turned to her and ever-so-gently screamed, **"WHAT'S JUNIOR'S PHONE NUMBER? WE NEED TO CALL JUNIOR AND WE NEED TO CALL HIM NOW!!"**

Wall Street smiled as she reached for her cell phone. "I thought you'd never ask."

* * * * *

Once again Wall Street and I walked through the dark, narrow, and this time very windy alley to visit Junior the Whiz Kid Genius.

Once again we headed down the steep, scary steps. And, once again we banged on the cold, creepy door.

"Who is present?" a tiny voice squeaked from the other side of the door.

"It's us," Wall Street answered.

After about a hundred *clicks* of locks being unlocked, and *clanks* of bolts being unbolted (plus the usual *chatter-chatter-chatter* of my teeth), the door finally

*CREEEEEEAK*ed

open.

Inside, it was even darker and spookier. I don't want to say it was scary, but on the Creep-You-Out Scale of 1–10, I'd definitely give it an 11.

"Hello?" Wall Street called into the darkness.

No answer.

She tried again. "Hello?"

"Good afternoon," a tiny little voice whispered.

"AUGHHH!"

my tiny little courage screamed.

But Wall Street wasn't frightened. No sir, not with her courage (and hunger for money). "Hey, Junior, how come it's so dark?" she complained. "We can't do business in the dark."

"Shhh," the tiny voice whispered. At last the lights came on. Beside us stood a kid wearing glasses and sipping a mug of hot chocolate. He was barely seven years old. He stuck out his hand for me to shake and continued, "I am extremely pleased that you have decided to pursue my offer, Mr. McDoogle."

(He may have looked seven, but he sounded seventy.)

"Why are we whispering?" Wall Street asked.

"It is Tina," Junior said. He started forward and motioned us to follow. We approached a stack of metal cages. In them were an assortment

of animals—rats, mice, hamsters, guinea pigs . . .
plus a few dozen worms, snails, and cockroaches
thrown in just to make things more interesting.

But Junior wasn't concerned with them.
Instead, he stopped in front of a cage that held
a single, large tarantula.

**WARNING: If you have a thing about spiders,
stop reading this immediately. (And while you're
at it, pray I can stop living it.)**

**ADDITIONAL WARNING: If you have a thing about
spiders and still bought this title with the creepy
cover, stop reading this immediately and go see a
psychiatrist. (But keep praying for me.)**

"What's wrong with her?" I asked.
"Sweet Tina appears to be depressed."
"How can you tell?"
"Step closer and examine her facial features."
I moved closer to the cage and squinted
inside. All I saw were the usual creepy spider
eyes, creepy legs, creepy jaw, and—

"Tee-hee, tee-hee."

"What was that?" Wall Street asked.

"I am uncertain," Junior said. "Though it appears to be coming from—"

"Hee-hee, hee-hee."

"Why, that is most remarkable."

"What?" I asked.

"It is coming from Tina." He turned to me in surprise and continued. "Your presence appears to be relieving her depression and making her

"Ha-ha, ho-ho."

giggle and laugh."

"He has that effect on lots of girls." Wall Street smirked. "Just ask Megan Melkner."

Suddenly, Tina really began yucking it up. Then she rolled onto her back and began kicking her legs in the air,

"hee-hee"-ing, "ha-ha"-ing, and "ho-ho"-ing

so hard, she could barely breathe.

"This is most remarkable," Junior said. "Perhaps it is your scent."

"My what?"

"He says you stink," Wall Street said.

"No way." I frowned. "I showered just last month. Or was it the month before?"

But Junior wasn't listening. "This is a world-changing breakthrough of staggering consequ—"

"Listen," Wall Street interrupted. "I'm all for world-changing breakthroughs, but can we get on with it?"

Junior looked up from the cage and asked, "*It?*"

"You know, making those great green gobs of cold, hard cash?"

He scowled slightly. "Making money, is that all you care about?"

"No, of course not. I care about counting it, too!"

"Actually," I said, "we are in kind of a hurry."

"Very well." Junior pushed up his glasses and led us to the other side of the room. "Allow me to present the experiment with which you will be assisting."

With that, he pulled aside a huge curtain to reveal an even huger computer. Talk about impressive. This thing had more flashing lights than a Christmas tree gone berserk. Directly beside it sat an old-fashioned barber chair—except this chair had metal clamps to hold down your arms and legs—and a giant football helmet that hung down on an electric cable. On the helmet's side and top were all sorts of control knobs and electrode-thingies.

"What is it?" I asked.

Junior grinned. "It is my Giant Occipital Organ Fortifier."

"Your what?"

"I refer to it as my 'G.O.O.F.' for short."

I threw Wall Street a nervous look.

"What's it do?" she asked.

"It magnifies the molecular makeup within the various neurons and synaptic pathways, thereby—"

"Whoa, whoa, whoa," Wall Street interrupted. "Any chance of having that in English?"

"Certainly." He cleared his throat and tried again. "It, uh, duh, like makes you, uh, not so dumb by, um, uh, don't tell me—" (It was nice to see even brainiacs can have a sense of humor.) "Oh, yeah, by, uh, making your brain, um, a bunch more bigger."

"Well, why didn't you say so?" Wall Street answered.

Junior shook his head, then walked us to another set of cages. "However, as can be observed from these recent experiments, my success has been somewhat limited."

I bent down and looked into the first cage.

Nothing but more rats. Except these little crit-
ters had noses like elephants!

"Yikes!" I gasped.

Junior nodded. "Instead of magnifying their
brains, my G.O.O.F. enlarged their noses."

I don't want to hurt their feelings, so let's
just say they were gross in a mad-scientist-
gone-crazy sort of way.

Wall Street was at another cage. "What's
with these guys?" she asked. It was full of your
everyday guinea pigs—except that they had lips
the size of doughnuts!

Junior sighed wearily. "My most recent
attempt. But instead of enlarging their minds
my G.O.O.F. enlarged their—"

"Lips," I said, taking a half step back. "You
gave them giant lips!"

"I am afraid so."

"So how do I fit in?" I asked, already fearing
the worst.

"The problem does not lie with my G.O.O.F.,
but with the subjects."

"You mean the rats and guinea pigs?" I
asked.

"Precisely. The machine was designed for
humans. These are merely rodents."

"So . . ." I took a nervous gulp.

"So the time has come to experiment on a real person."

I'd like to say I was going to be surprised, but I've lived through enough of these stories to guess what was next. I felt myself going cold. I felt myself growing numb. I felt myself not wanting to ask the question I knew I had to ask, so I asked it, anyway. "So, you want to use me as . . ."

". . . my next test subject."

I started backing up. "No way." I shook my head. "Absolutely not. Forget it!"

"But—"

I turned to Wall Street. "Tell him!" I exclaimed. "Tell him it's not possible!"

"I'm afraid Wally's right," she said.

I nodded, grateful for the support, thankful that Wall Street was taking my side. Unfortunately, she wasn't quite finished. . . .

"At least not for the price you quoted me over the phone."

"Wall Street!" I cried.

She shrugged. "For something like this, we'll have to charge a little extra."

Chapter 4

Dumbo Jr.

So there we stood in Junior's lab as Wall Street argued over the cost of my life. I was touched by her love and devotion as she insisted on more than $5.00, on more than $10.00—in fact, I bet we could have gotten up to $14.95 if Junior hadn't said, "Remember, if the G.O.O.F. works and enlarges his mind, he may invest intelligently for you in the stock market and—"

"—make me a ton more dough!" Wall Street cried.

"Precisely."

"All right!" Wall Street shouted, grabbing his hand and shaking it. "We've got a deal!"

Of course, they also allowed me to express my opinion—which I did by quietly turning, running toward the door, and screaming . . .

"SOMEBODY SAVE ME!"

I almost made it to safety, except for those three or four walls I slammed into. Then, of course, there was that huge stack of worm trays I

*K-rash*ed

into, causing about half of them to fall on top of me. Fortunately, when the trays fell, instead of guinea pigs or whatever, nothing but worms spilled out. Unfortunately, I was knocked too unconscious to appreciate the difference.

When I woke up, Wall Street was helping Junior carry me toward the G.O.O.F. while speaking such comforting words as, "Don't worry, Wally, even if it fails, think how much money we'll get to pay for your funeral."

I don't like being a spoilsport, but I figured now was as good a time as any to fight for my life. Immediately, I began some karate, then tae kwon do, then the greatest self-defense of them all . . . crying for my mommy!

Despite my heroic efforts (along with my usual begging and sobbing), they managed to get me to the chair. But I'd twisted and squirmed until I was upside down.

"Buckle him in!" Junior cried.

"But he's upside down!" Wall Street shouted.

"With my numerous failed attempts, I doubt it should make any difference."

With that bit of encouraging news, Wall Street did what any true-blue friend would do. She walked up to him, she looked him squarely in the eyes, and she said, "Okay."

Immediately, they began clamping my arms down in the leg clamps and my legs up in the arm clamps. "What about this?" she asked as she reached for the football helmet that hung from the electrical cable. "Where do we put it?"

"It makes no difference," he said as I continued squirming and kicking. He reached for the "ON" switch and continued, "As I previously mentioned, I seriously doubt that anything positive will—"

"AUGHHH!"
K-kick

The "AUGHHH!" was, of course, yours truly, screaming his head off.

The *K-kick* was my foot flying and hitting the helmet.

Oh, yeah, and there was one other sound . . .

kuuuzch-kuuuzch-kuuuzch

That, dear reader, is the sound a kicked G.O.O.F. helmet makes when it starts swinging back and forth and all the rays that are supposed to be shooting into the brain start shooting around the room. No problem except for

kuuuzch . . . K-Blamb!
blub, blub, blub

turning Junior's mug of hot chocolate into a giant hot tub of hot chocolate. Or

kuuuzch . . . K-Pow!

turning a nearby pencil into a giant log. Or

kuuuzch . . . K-Blewie!

turning all those floating dust particles into huge asteroids that started

"Look out!"

crashing into the floor, leaving huge

K-bamb, K-bamb, K-bamb

craters wherever they hit.

"Stop fighting!" Wall Street shouted at me.
"This will only hurt for a moment!"

Somehow, I wasn't encouraged. I kept fighting and squirming until I—

K-*KICK*ed

the helmet so hard that it swung way out to the
side and suddenly—

kuuuzch-kuuuzch-kuuuzch
squirm, squirm . . . slither, slither . . .

Remember those escaping worms that I said
were no problem a while back?

Well, now they were a problem.

Only, they weren't exactly worms. Not anymore. Now they were like giant snakes, a hundred
feet long, slithering across the floor toward us!

And if that wasn't bad enough, there was
also the obnoxious

*smack, smack, smack*ing

of their mouths or jaws or whatever giant earthworms smack when they're about to enjoy a fine
dining experience.

Then, just when we were about to become

earthworm appetizers (making this the shortest *My Life As . . .* book in history), they slithered directly into the path of the falling asteroids. So instead of *squirm, squirm . . . slither, slither,* we were now greeted with

Squish, Squish
Splatter, Splatter.

Gross? You bet.
Messy? The worst.
But worth it, if you like to live.
Which I did.
Which I might have.
Which I would have . . . if Wall Street hadn't taken advantage of my distraction, flipped me around in the chair, and slapped the helmet on my head.
"Okay, Junior!" she yelled. "Hit it!"
Junior turned the switch and

kuuuzch-kuuuzch-kuuuzch

the rays, or whatever they were, shot out of the helmet and into my brain. Well, that's what they were supposed to do. Unfortunately, they hit a little detour along the way . . .
My little ears.

Only they weren't so little anymore. Because with each

kuuuzch-kuuuzch-kuuuzch

(and there were about fifty of them), my ears grew about an inch.

Now, I'm no math genius, but if you take fifty *kuuuzch-kuuuzch-kuuuzch*es and multiply them times one inch, you'll get ears the size of—don't tell me, I'll figure this out. Uh . . . 1 inch x 50 is . . . uh, er . . . Well, let's just say it's not bad if you're planning to dress up like Dumbo the elephant for Halloween, or if you don't mind looking like you've got satellite dishes stuck to your head. But if you want to pass as a normal human being, you might get a little, oh, I don't know . . .

"AUGHHHHHH!"

freaked.

The good news was, the helmet could no longer contain my head (or at least my ears), so it

K-Blewie!-ed.

The bad news was, I finally broke free of the barber chair and raced out the door.

And why is that bad news, you ask? (You are asking, right?)

It's bad news because . . . remember that windy alley I talked about outside Junior's door? Well, once I got outside and started running down it, the wind began whipping my ears. No problem until they started lifting me off the ground! At first I rose only a few inches, then a few feet, and then . . . well, let's just say I quickly became the world's first living human hang glider!

Actually, it wasn't too bad. Almost fun. Of course, it would have been more fun if I could have somehow controlled where I was going.

Which I couldn't.

Which explains the

ZZZ . . . ZZZ
crackle-crackle
smoke-smoke

I heard (and smelled) when my pants leg brushed against the overhead electrical wires.

No problem, except for the part about my pants catching fire.

MY PANTS CATCHING FIRE?!

(Sorry, I'm yelling again, aren't I?)

So there I was, sailing above the street with pants flaming like one of Dad's backyard barbecues. But, being a fairly intelligent person (or at least knowing how to fake it), I reached back and tried smacking out the flames.

Unfortunately, all that smacking caused more ear flapping, and I really started to gain altitude. In fact, before I knew it, I was so high that

K-WOOOOOOO—
"AUGHHHH!"
—OOOOOOSHHHH

I was playing tag with jet airliners!

Actually, it wasn't tag. It was more like badminton. But instead of using those little birdie things, we were using

K-WOOOOOOO—
"AUGHHHHH!"
—OOOOOOSHHHH

dink!

K-WOOOOOOO—
"AUGHHHHH!"
—OOOOOOSHHHH
dink!

me!

But they weren't the only ones who wanted
to play. Word quickly spread, and soon I was
visited by a couple of

Wooosh!
Wooosh!

fighter jets.

They seemed kinda friendly. In fact, they
didn't even bat me around. No sir. Instead, they
were more interested in shooting me down!

SHOOTING ME DOWN??!!

(Yes, I'm yelling again, but it's hard hearing
over the noise of fighter jets shooting warning
shots.)

**FIGHTER JETS SHOOTING WARNING
SHOTS??!!**

(Sorry.)

The best I could figure, they were a little nervous about me being up there. Which was fine,
'cause I was a bit nervous myself. Soon, the
planes began circling me, the pilots motioning
through the cockpit with their hands. As best I
could tell, they wanted me to grab the ends of my
ears and pull them down. Not a bad idea since
this would definitely stop them from being wings.

So, wanting to keep the guys happy (and me

alive), I reached out, grabbed my ears, and pulled them straight down.

I tell you, the guys knew exactly what they were talking about. Because just as soon as I pulled down my ears, I quit flying.

Good.

There was only one problem.

As soon as I quit flying, I started

"A
 U
  U
   U
    U
     U
      G
       H
        H
         !
          !"

falling.

Chapter 5

Sealed Lips

So there I was doing my world-famous "Auuuuughh!! I'm going to die! Auuuuughh!! I'm going to die!" routine (You know, the one where my life flashes before my eyes?) when, suddenly, everything flashed just a little differently.

Flash 1. I saw all the work I'd gone through trying to fix Mom's vase 'cause I wouldn't tell her the truth and take responsibility for my actions.

Flash 2. I saw all the worry I'd gone through trying to fix Mom's vase 'cause I wouldn't tell her the truth and take responsibility for my actions.

Flash 3. I saw all the pain I'd gone through trying to fix Mom's vase 'cause I wouldn't tell her the truth and take responsibility for my actions.

Call me overly intelligent, but I was starting to see a pattern.

Call me overly ignorant, but I refused to believe it.

So there I was, hanging on to my ears and falling to the earth just faster than the speed of light, when I suddenly had a brilliant idea . . .

If hanging on to my ears causes me to fall, there must be something I can do to cause me to stop. After careful calculations and seconds of research, I decided to try a radical approach. I decided to let go of my ears.

I know, I know, it was a courageous move on my part, but desperate times call for desperate dorkiness.

Because the decision was so frightening, I had to work up my courage by counting to three.

"One: Okay, McDoogle, here goes. Deep breaths, now . . .

"Two: Don't worry, you've done all the calculations . . .

"Thr—"

K-Rash!

This, of course, is the sound of a big-eared body hitting hard-packed earth . . . when it took too long to count to three.

The nice thing about unconsciousness is you don't remember those long, boring rides in the ambulance, those monotonous hours on the operating table, or all those little-kid sing-along videos Mom plays for you when you're at home recovering.

But all good things must come to an end. When I finally woke up, I noticed two things. First, my ears had shrunk back to normal. Second, I was greeted with many kind, sensitive questions, including:

"WHAT WERE YOU THINKING?!"

That, of course, would be Dad. He gets a little upset when he, uh, gets upset.

Then, there was Mom:

"Would you like to pop in another video so we can all sing along?"

And, finally, dear, sweet, little Carrie:

"Give me twenty bucks for keeping my mouth shut about the vase." (She'd obviously been taking lessons from Wall Street.)

Here I'd gone through all this pain and misery, but I was no closer to solving the vase problem than when I started. Of course, I could have confessed right then and there. I could have told Mom the truth and taken responsibility for my actions. But then I wouldn't get to enjoy all the upcoming pain and misery.

It was a tough decision—to be destroyed or

not to be destroyed, that is the question. But since I've never scored high on learning from my mistakes and since we were only halfway through this book, I voted for keeping my mouth shut. Yes sir, some pain is just too good to pass up.

So, instead of doing the right thing, I grabbed Ol' Betsy and passed away the hours by working on my superhero story. . . .

When we last left our burper buddy, Burping Boy (or is it burping buddy, Burper Boy?), he was busy watching the sinisterly sinister and startling stupendous (or is it startling sinister and sinisterly stupendous——)

"Hey, can we just, *burp,* get on with it, please?"

"Who . . . who said that?" I type.

"Me."

"'Me' who?" I type.

"Me, your superhero."

"You can't talk, you're just an imaginary character."

"And by the looks of things, *burp,* you can't write."

"Sorry, I'm just a little, I don't know . . . pre-occupied."

"Whoa, 'preoccupied.' Pretty fancy word for a kid. But then again, writers use big words and you're serious about this writer thing, aren't you?"

"Yeah."

"And I'm serious about this superhero business, so can we get on with the story—or are you going to keep worrying about your mom's vase?"

"How do you know about the vase?"

"I'm your imagination. Where you go, I go."

"Everywhere?"

"Yup."

"Like, even to the bathroom?"

"That's the way it works."

"*Eewww.*"

"Tell me about it. Now, about the story? I don't want to complain, but remember that dust bunny you had growing under my bed?"

"Yeah," I type.

"Well, now it's the size of a—

ROAR

grizzly bear."

"What happened to his giggles? He's supposed to giggle."

"Hey, it's your story, not mine.
All I know is——"

ROOOOOAAAAR

"You know what I said about grizzly
bears?"

"Yeah?"

"Forget it. Now we're talking the
size of a small tree. In fact, he's
starting to grow through my ceiling!"

"But——"

"Can we PLEASE get on with this,
before he breaks through my——"

RIP, CRASH
Bang, Blam
Clatter, Clatter, Clatter.

"Never mind."

"Sorry."

"He's still growing...."

"Oh, right. Here goes, then."

Suddenly, the giant dust bunny
bursts through the roof and is now
the size of...the size of——

"A GIANT tree!"

"Right."

Suddenly, the dust bunny has grown to the size of a giant tree. But this is no concern for Burping Boy. Taking a giant swig of ginger ale, he builds up maximum burp pressure, points his head to the ground, lets forth a giant

BURP!

and takes off like a rocket, shooting through the hole in his roof. Then, with a series of smaller

burp, burp...burp...burp,
burp, burps

he makes midcourse corrections until he's face-to-face with the dreaded creature.

"Hold it, dust bunnies don't have faces. They're just—"

"Excuse me?" I type.

"You just wrote, 'face-to-face.' But they don't have faces. They're just fluffy bunches of dust that stick together under beds and—"

"Excuse me, I'm on a roll. Would you mind letting me write?"

"Yeah, but——"

"Just stick to your superhero business."

"What business? Looking into the face of a stupid dust bunny? Not exactly the thrill of my life——"

Suddenly, the giant dust bunny opens its mouth and roars with such force that it throws our hero across the street——

"Much more interesting."

"Thanks."

Then, racing back across the street he

HONK! HONK! HON——

narrowly misses being hit by a giant semitruck.

"That was close. Thanks."

"Don't mention it."

He arrives just in time to see his bad bunny buddy hop from his yard and stomp onto the neighbor's house. But how is that possible? How can mere dust particles form a real-life bunny,

let alone make it strong enough to
crunch other people's houses?

"Exactly." Our hero complains.
"That's what I've been saying. What
you're writing is totally unrealis—"

When, suddenly—

Piiiissssshhhhhh
Piiiiissssshhhhhh

our heroic hero hears a horribly hor-
rific sound hovering high over the
hopping hare in a huge helicopter.

"I hope your readers don't sprain
their tongues."

I continue typing: And inside that
helicopter...

(Da-Da-Daaaaa....)

"Finally, the bad-guy music."
"That's right."
And inside that helicopter is...

(Da-Da-Daaaaa...)

"You just did that."

"Do you mind?"

And inside that helicopter is the baddest of bad boys—

"Yes..."

—the fiendish of fiends—

"Yes, yes..."

—the evilest of evildoers—

"Yes, go on..."

Hair Spray Dude!

"Oh, brother, is that the best you could come up with?"

Suddenly, our hero understands why the dust bunny has such strength, why it doesn't fall apart like normal dust bunnies.

"Why is that?"

Because, from the giant tanks strapped to the helicopter's side, the vile villain is spraying sticky hair spray! No wonder the bunny is so strong and stiff!

Looking up into the sky, Burping Boy cries, "Hair Spray Dude, is that you?!"

"That's right, Belching Bum."

"Are you the one giving all the strength to that dust bunny?"

"And not just that one!" the bad guy shouts. "Between the stickiness

of this spray (plus a little growth
hormone I've thrown in for good measure), dust bunnies around the world
will crawl out from under their beds
to take control. Soon, there will be
no place to hide. Soon, there will—

Ring . . .

"What's that?"
"It's, uh, my phone," I type.

Ring . . .

"Another interruption?"
"Sorry, but I should really . . .

Ring . . .

answer it."

Ring . . .

"All right, go ahead."
"What's the problem?" Hair Spray
Dude shouts from his helicopter.
"It's our author," Burping Boy
yells. "He's got to answer his phone."

"In the middle of our story?" Hair
Spray Dude scorns. "You're kidding?"

"Wish I was!" Burping Boy shouts.
"It's been like this the whole story
long."

I wanted to stick around and defend myself,
but I had a phone to answer. I picked up the
receiver and said, "Hello?"

"Hey, Wally, how you feeling?"

"Wall Street?"

"Listen, I got another great moneymaking
plan."

"I, uh . . ." I hesitated as I looked down at my
recovering body. "I don't think that's such a good
ide—"

"Great, I'll be right over. Oh, and don't
worry, this one is completely safe!"

Chapter 6

Reunion Time

I'd barely stepped outside when I noticed the giant banner that Wall Street was putting in my front yard:

Wally's Dumbo-Ear Flying School

Yes, as the role model for care and compassion, Wall Street had already found a way to cash in on my pain and suffering. There was just one problem. . . .

"Hey, what happened to your ears?!" she cried.

"They shrank down to normal."

"They can't do that. Stretch them back!"

"Why?"

"Look at the sign. Stretch 'em back! Stretch 'em back!"

She seemed pretty upset so, to keep her happy, I gave my ears a little tug.

Nothing.

She reached over and gave them a giant tug.

More of nothing—well, except for incredible pain.

"OW! What'd you do that for?"

"How do you expect me to run Wally's Dumbo-Ear Flying School if you don't have Dumbo ears?"

"The same way you can run a flying school if I can't fly."

"You can't fly, either?!"

I stuck my head into the breeze. I tilted it to the left, then to the right. I even bounced it up and down for a little ear-flapping action. "Nope," I said, "nothing."

"That's just great," she moaned. "Who in their right mind would buy flying lessons from someone who can't fly!"

A voice interrupted from behind. "Excuse, *snap-snap,* me."

It sounded eerily familiar. I felt my face twitch once, twice, then—

"Hello, *pop-pop,* Wallace."

Trying to be polite, I cranked up my best

grin and turned to see, you guessed it, Megan Melkner. There she stood, in all of her grinning glory, batting those baby blues, snapping that Chewie Blewie, and, of course, giggling . . . lots and lots of giggling.

"Megan," I croaked. "What, *twitch*, brings you, *twitch-twitch*, here?"

"I want to learn to fly."

"Didn't you hear what I just told Wall Street? I *can't* fly."

"That's okay," she sighed dreamily.

"So . . . ," I said, trying to swallow. But my mouth had grown as dry as a cotton ball in the Sahara under a heat lamp. ". . . if I can't teach you to fly, what can I do for you?"

She produced a twenty-dollar bill. "You can take my money."

"For what?"

"For letting me stand in your presence."

Repeat in the twitch department. "But—"

"Sold!" Wall Street said, snatching the money from her hand. "At a buck a minute, that means you can stand there for twenty minutes!"

"*For* what?!" I repeated.

"For a taste of heaven," Megan sighed.

My twitchings went into overtime. I tried to protest, but it did no good. Between Megan's wanting to spend money and Wall Street's wanting to take it, I was outnumbered. So there we stood for twenty minutes in my front yard doing absolutely nothing. Well, nothing except *snapping, sighing, . . .* and *twitching.*

"Time's up!" Wall Street finally cried.

"Thank you so very much," Megan said, shaking my hand. Then, turning toward her house, she just sort of floated off in a dreamlike state.

"Same time tomorrow?" Wall Street shouted.

"You, *snap-sigh,* bet, *pop* (sigh*)*!"

I dropped my head into my hands. "No way," I mumbled.

"Why not?" Wall Street asked.

I looked back up. "Because some things are more important than money."

Wall Street frowned, the concept obviously new to her. "It's either work with her or go back to Junior Whiz Kid."

(Of course, there was a third option—something about telling Mom what happened, but that was too intelligent to be considered.)

"Junior's still talking to you?" I asked.

"Calling every day. He's got another experiment he wants you to try."

"Forget it!" I shook my head. "No way. Absolutely not."

"Excuse me!" Megan turned and called from

the end of the block. "If I bring fifty dollars tomorrow, can I stay fifty minutes?"

"You bet!" Wall Street shouted. "In fact, tomorrow we have a two-for-one special—you pay two hundred dollars and you can stay for one hundred minutes!"

"Wow!" Megan squealed in excitement. "Sign me up!" With that, she turned to *snap, pop,* and *sigh* herself all the way home.

I snickered at Wall Street's foolishness. "Two hundred dollars? Where on earth is some girl going to get two hundred dollars?"

"Thought you knew. Her dad's a gazillionaire. He gives her all the money she wants."

My smile dropped as fast as my twitchings resumed. Without a word, I grabbed Wall Street's cell phone.

"What are you doing?" she asked.

"I'm calling Junior Whiz Kid!"

* * * * *

An hour later we were back in Junior's creepy lab, walking past the cages of creepy rats, creepy mice, creepy hamsters, creepy cockroaches, and—

clink-clink-clink

"What's that?" I asked.

"It is Tina," Junior said. He motioned us toward the tarantula's cage. "I have treated her skin with a special chemical that has hardened it to the strength of steel."

clink-clink-clink

I stooped down and peered into the cage. It was the same old Tina. But now, as she paced back and forth, she was

*clink-clink-clink*ing.

Junior continued, "Of course, it has not helped in her depression, but she—"

clink-clink-clink
"Tee-hee, tee-hee."

Suddenly, he stopped. "Why, that is most remarkable. She is starting to laugh again. Mr. McDoogle, please come closer."

I moved in even closer, and sure enough, her laughing—

"Ho-ho, ha-ha."

grew louder. Louder and harder until she once
again rolled over onto her back—

clink-clank-clunk

and kicked up her legs, having the time of her—

clink-"hee"
clank-"ho"
clunk-"ha"

life.

Of course, I was pleased to provide such hap-
piness (especially when it didn't involve any
body part breakage), but Junior had other
things on his mind.

So did Wall Street. "What do you want him
to do, and how much money are you paying us?"
she asked.

He headed over to a larger cage. "I am afraid
I have a very grave problem." Inside the cage
was a snail. But not your everyday, garden-
variety snail. Oh, no. This snail was the size of
your everyday, garden-variety . . . St. Bernard!
(But without the slobbers. Snail slime, yes, but
no slobbers.)

"Wow!" Wall Street gasped.

"What happened?" I asked.

"Do you recall when you kicked the G.O.O.F. helmet and the beam shot into the worm trays?"

"Yes."

"Apparently, a few rays struck this poor creature as well. But the question is, why have your ears returned to normal and he has not?"

"So, how can I help?" I asked, feeling that old familiar fear for my life.

"I should like to re-create last week's experiment and examine what exactly transpired."

"I, uh . . ." I swallowed. "I don't think so."

"Wally's right," Wall Street agreed.

I sighed in relief.

Junior took a half step toward me. "If you would just allow me to strap you into that chair one more time and—"

I started backing up. "No way."

"But it would only be—"

"Forget it," Wall Street said. She stepped between us. "You heard my client. Last week's experience was much too frightening for him!"

"I'll pay the same price," Junior offered.

"Absolutely not!" Wall Street answered. She turned to me and grinned, obviously proud of her growth as a human being. "Some things are more important than money. Isn't that right, Wally?"

I nodded so hard my head nearly flew off.

She turned back to Junior and said, "Sorry, no sale."

To which Junior replied, "I'll pay double the price."

To which Wall Street turned back to me, lunged in my direction, and cried, "GRAB HIM!"

Of course, I used all of my great athletic ability to get away—which means they caught me in about 2.3 seconds. But I wouldn't give up so easily, no sir. As someone inclined to living, I did what anyone inclined to living would do. I squirmed and kicked and screamed like a baby.

Unfortunately, the kicking and screaming did no good.

Unfortunatelier (don't try that word on your English teacher), the squirming did.

In one unsmooth move, I spun free from them and stumbled away. That was the good news. The bad news was, I stumbled directly into the giant snail cage.

No problem, except I hit it so hard, the door sprang open.

Again, no problem . . . except Ol' Snail Buddy decided it was time to make a break for it.

Now, snails may not be the fastest creatures in the world, but they are strong and, as I mentioned, slimy. My point is, nothing slowed him:

Not Junior's attempt to stop him . . .

"Eewww, ick, I have stepped into his slime!" he cried while desperately wiping his feet.

Not Wall Street's attempt at being a hero . . .

"I'm so outta here!"

Not even the . . .

K-BAMB!

back door that the critter broke through as he headed into the alley.

"STOP HIM!" Junior cried, still trying to wipe off his feet. "DO NOT LET HIM ESCAPE!"

But, of course, he did escape. Big time!

Chapter 7

Ride 'em, Snail Boy!

So there we were, chasing Junior's giant snail down the alley. Actually, "chasing" isn't the right word, since it was moving as slow as, well, as a snail.

"Hey! Hey!" Junior cried, banging on the snail's shell, trying to get him to turn. But the critter wasn't listening.

I decided to use another method—persuading him with my incredible charm and dashing good looks. (Hey, everybody needs a little fantasy.) "Here, snaily, snaily, snaily."

Unfortunately, my success rated as high as Junior's: zero.

Then, suddenly, I heard:

"crunch, crunch, crunch . . .

Wally, *belch,* is that you?"

Now, for you newbies, that is the voice (and sound effects) of my other best friend, Opera, the human eating machine. Yes sir, Opera has three great loves in his life: eating junk food, listening to opera, and, uh, eating more junk food.

I looked up and spotted him coming down the alley. "Opera! What are you doing here?"

"Wall Street said you were down this way. What's up?"

"Nothing." I shrugged. "Just your typical snail wrangling."

"Belch." He nodded. "Need a hand?"

"Don't know what you can do," I said, putting my back against the snail and pushing with all of my strength (which was like pushing with nothing at all).

"Here," Opera said, *"crunch, crunch, crunch,* let me—

BURP!

(Wow, that was a good one. Now you
know my inspiration for Burping Boy.)

try."

With that, Opera tossed aside his current bag of Chippy Chipper potato chips (don't worry, he has two or three others strapped to his side for emergencies), wiped his mouth, and then the most remarkable thing happened.

As he wiped his mouth, crumbs and salt fell onto the road right in front of Snail Buddy. Crumbs and salt that caused the creature to suddenly freak, spin around, and find the quickest way out of there.

Unfortunately, the quickest way out was not around, but up. Up, as in up the side of the nearest building!

"Opera! What did you do?" I cried.

"Got, *belch,* me!" he shouted. "I just—"

"It is the salt!" Junior yelled. "Salt kills snails. He is running from the salt!"

Now, it's one thing to have a giant snail inching down a dark alley where no one can see him (or blame you). It's quite another when he starts climbing up buildings in plain view of the world (and people who will probably tell your parents). That's why I figured I'd end my career of trying to help and begin something entirely different . . . like spinning around and running for my life.

"Wally!" Junior shouted. "Do not depart from—"

SLIP
"Whoa!"

"AUGHHH . . ."

The *SLIP* was me sliding on the snail's slimy path.

The "Whoa!" was me flying into the air.

And the "AUGHHH"? That was me grabbing on to something, anything, so I wouldn't crash headfirst onto the pavement. Unfortunately, the "anything" just happened to be the snail's two antennae.

"Wally, release him!" Junior cried. "Release him!"

But I couldn't release him. The reason was obvious to any snail slime expert. But if you're not an expert, let me explain:

There are two types of slime . . .

Slippery—as in a snail trail
Sticky—as in a snail body

And since these particular antennae were attached to this particular snail body, that made them . . . you guessed it, sticky. So sticky that it took all of my strength (which we've already determined is none) just to free my hands. Unfortunately, by the time I got them loose, we'd climbed so high that if I let go I'd plummet (as in skydive without a parachute) to some very bad bodily injuries. And since I'm allergic to broken body parts, I decided to hang on to those antennae as we kept crawling higher and higher and . . . well, you get the picture.

The good news was, not many folks noticed. Just a couple dozen shoppers. Of course, they started screaming. You know, the usual stuff like:

> "A giant snail and a boy are
>   climbing that building!"
> "A giant snail and a boy are
>   climbing that building!"

And, not wanting this latest disaster to get back to my folks, which would mean:

—telling them about Junior, which would mean
—telling them why I needed the money, which would mean
—telling them the truth about the vase.

I did my best to calm the shoppers by making it look like I was just some kid fooling around. I climbed onto the critter's back and pretended to be riding him cowboy-style. "Yee-haa!" I cried, slapping the back of his shell with my hand. "Get along, little snaily! Get along!"

But the crowd wasn't buying it . . . which would explain their mass hysteria (not to mention their mass faintings.) But a dozen passed-out shoppers wasn't so bad. At least no one had called the police or—

"THIS IS THE POLICE!" a voice blasted through a megaphone. "RELEASE THAT SNAIL AND COME DOWN WITH YOUR HANDS UP!"

I glanced down at the street. By now we were seven or eight stories up, and the view was terrific. Unfortunately, that view also included five or six police cars skidding to a stop—along with a fire truck and an ambulance (no doubt ready to collect any falling snails . . . or bodies).

"It's okay," I told myself. "The police are here to help. Your folks still don't have to know. I mean, it's not like you're going to wind up on the six o'clock news or anything, so just—"

WHOP WHOP **WHOP WHOP**

I looked over my shoulder and saw, you guessed it, the Channel 2 News

WHOP **WHOP WHOP WHOP**

helicopter approaching and hovering beside us!

Ever have one of those days?

(Unfortunately, I have one of those lives.)

"Hey, Wally!" Opera shouted from below. "Looks like you're going to be, *belch,* famous!"

But famous was the last thing I wanted—especially if it meant my folks finding out. So I kept my face turned away from the camera. That way no one could recognize me. Well, almost no one . . .

"Hey, Wally!" a voice shouted from above.

I looked up and saw Wall Street sticking her head out of a window just above me. "How's it going?" she shouted.

"Oh, I don't know." I shrugged. "Pretty good . . . well, except for this giant snail climbing up this building, and those police cars, and that helicopter, and—"

"Don't worry," she yelled. "I've got the perfect solution."

I wanted to point out that her "perfect solution" had gotten me into this trouble in the first place, but the helicopter was much

WHOP WHOP WHOP WHOP

closer and I had to keep my face hidden.

"Listen!" she continued. "I've got Chef Pierre here in the room beside me!"

"A chef?!" I yelled. "You've got the wrong guy! Opera's down below in the alley!"

"No, no, no. Pierre is a *French* chef."

"So?"

"So, French chefs love escargot."

"Escar—what?!" I yelled.

"Es-car-GO! Snails! They love to cook and eat snails! I told him how big your pal there is and he 'bout had a heart attack. He's going to pay me a ton of money for him."

Of course, nothing thrilled me more than helping Wall Street make money—unless, of course, it was living. But, before I could point this out, I heard:

"Très magnifique! C'est bon!"

The language definitely wasn't English. I stole a quick peek up, and sure enough, there was some French chef with a tall white hat, busily smacking his lips.

But I wasn't the only one who noticed. Apparently, my overgrown Snail Buddy also recognized the accent. Suddenly, his head raised to look . . . just as Chef Pierre produced a giant cleaver and began sharpening it in anticipation of the feast.

. . . a feast that Snail Buddy was in no mood to be a part of. Immediately, his antennae shot straight up, and immediatelier (that's another one you don't want to try on your English teacher), he escaped by doing a 180 and leaping off the wall.

A good plan, except for the "leaping off the wall" part. Not being the brightest of creatures, he hadn't bothered figuring that if you leap off a wall that you're stuck to, the chances of returning to that wall aren't so great. In fact, the chances of

"AUGHHHHHHH!"

falling are pretty high.

But, even as I hurled toward my death (or at least another lengthy visit to unconsciousness), I knew my secret about the vase was safe. Mom would never find out what I was doing. She'd never know I was here. All I had to do was keep my face toward the wall and away from the TV camera in the helicopter.

Which I almost did.

Well, except for the part where I hung on to Snail Buddy for dear life as we fell face-first past the helicopter. Yes sir, nothing brings fame like a nice big closeup of yours truly sailing by the camera

"AUGHHHHHHHH!"-ing

his little heart out.

Chapter 8

Will I Ever Learn? (probably not till chapter 10)

After the usual hospital stay, emergency operations, and home interrogations by my parents (where I gave nothing but my name, rank, and choice of videos to rewatch), things started to settle back to normal. . . .Well, except for the incredible guilt I had for not telling Mom about the broken vase . . . and the newscasts my brothers kept showing.

That's right! My brothers taped the newscast and took turns replaying the videos to torture me while I was stuck on the couch. But that was nothing compared to the 2.7 million copies Wall Street made and sold on the Internet for a mere $12.95 each (plus shipping and handling).

Of course, the TV news guys got things all mixed up. According to them, I wasn't falling with Snail Buddy, I was *flying* him. After all, wasn't I the Big-Eared Flying Boy who'd nearly been shot down by fighter jets the week before? I guess they just naturally figured I'd traded in my ears for a snail. Not only that, but they had the video to prove it—a nice big closeup of me and Snail Buddy flying past the camera, screaming our heads off.

But all the time there was that guilt I had for not telling Mom about the broken vase. Now, I don't know which was worse . . . my incredible guilt, or my incredible lack of intelligence. After all this, you'd think I'd learned my lesson and would tell the truth. You'd think I'd finally take responsibility and confess that I broke the vase. And that's what I planned to do . . . right after I earned enough money to buy another one so she'd never ever find out.

So much for learning lessons.

Unfortunately, class wasn't quite over . . .

A week or so later I was back to writing my superhero story. It was six in the morning. Nothing destroys a good night's sleep—or several —like guilt. And nothing drowns it out like a good story. So . . .

When we last left Burping Boy, he was in a sticky situation with the horrendously horrible and horrifically

inhospitable hoodlum hanging out in
the hovering helicopter (your tongue
tired yet?)——the one, the only...
Hair Spray Dude.

Now the fiendish fiend is spraying
hair spray on dust bunnies around the
world, turning the little balls of
dust into impossibly immense and
incredibly indestructible...(Uh...
um...does anybody have an "i" word
for monsters? No? Okay, moving on...)

No one's sure what made Hair Spray
Dude so horrible. Some say it was the
seven coats of hair spray his mother
used on him when getting him ready
for Sunday school.

Others insist it came from watching too many TV reporters whose plas-
ticized hair didn't move an inch when
they were reporting...even in hurri-
canes.

Finally, there's the ever-popular
notion that the smell simply reminded
him of his childhood (when his father
used hair spray instead of air freshener in the bathroom). And why would
any father use hair spray instead of
air freshener? Hey, who has time to

read labels when you're busy support-
ing a family and raising horrifically
inhospitable hoodlums?

Anyway, racing to the nearest fire-
box, our hero breaks the glass, throws
open the little door, and, instead of
setting off a fire alarm, pulls out a
giant bottle of ginger ale placed there
for just such superhero occasions.
Immediately, he

chug chug chugs

it down until he builds up the needed
burp pressure. Then, pointing his
head toward the ground, he once again
produces a distinguishingly dynamic
(though somewhat disgusting)

BURP!

which shoots him up faster than the
hand of some kid having to go to the
rest room.

But Hair Spray Dude is no fool. As
Burping Boy approaches, he simply
turns the spray nozzle to "ON" and
immediately

Piiiisssssshhhhhhh...

covers our hero with more hair spray
than those varnished helmet-heads you
see in all those political ads on TV.

Yet our hero will not be stopped.
"Give it up!" he shouts as he flies
toward the helicopter. "Mere hair
spray cannot stop me!"

"Good point, Burper Brat. But
maybe these three hundred pounds of
BBs will!" With that, Hair Spray Dude
pours out a giant barrel of BBs that
fall on top of Burping Boy.

Still, our hero isn't worried.
What can falling BBs do? Not much.
But, it isn't their falling that's
the problem. It's their sticking.
Soon he's covered from head to toe
with thousands of little BBs. And
what's wrong with that? Unfortunately, thousands of little BBs weigh
hundreds of extra pounds. And hundreds of extra pounds means Burping
Boy is no longer shooting up so fast.
In fact, he slows to a stop, and
actually starts to—

"Uh-oh."

"A

  U

    G

     H!"

Being the boasting bad boy that he is, Hair Spray can't resist shouting, "You might consider a weight-loss program. Those extra pounds can be hazardous to your health!" Then, making sure everyone gets the joke, he lets out his world-famous

"Moo-hoo-hoo, haa-ha!"

laugh.

But Burping Boy isn't worried. He may be racing toward the ground at a gazillion.7 miles an hour, but he's read enough of these superhero stories to know superheroes always win. More weight simply means he needs more burper power. So, with quiet confidence, he raises the bottle of ginger ale back to his lips and—

"Uhh...excuse me, Mr. Author?"

I try my best to ignore him and retype:

"With quiet confidence, he raises the
bottle of ginger ale back to his lips
and—"

"Excuse me?"

"Do we have to talk now?" I type. "I'm right
in the middle of an action sequence."

"Actually, that's the problem."

"And why is that a problem? You just drink
more ginger ale, burp harder, and shoot back
up."

"Except..."

"Except what?"

"Except the hair spray is so sticky
that I can't move my arms."

"So?"

"So, if I can't move my arms, I
can't drink the ginger ale. And if I
can't drink the ginger ale, I can't
burp. And if I can't burp, I can only
do one other thing."

"What's that?"

"I can only continue to
A
   U
    G
     H!
fall."

"What's the problem here?" Hair Spray Dude asks.

(Oh, brother, now everyone's into the act.)

"It's my arms," Burping Boy explains. "They're stuck to my side so I won't be able to drink the ginger ale and burp my way back for our fight scene."

"What?" Hair Spray Dude cries. "No fight scene!"

"Of course there'll be a fight scene," I type. "What's a superhero story without a fight scene?"

"Then let's get on with it!" Burping Boy shouts.

I nod, thinking as hard as I can. But no solution comes to mind.

"Excuse me!" Burping Boy yells. "I'm still falling and that ground is getting awfully close!"

"Yes, let's get going," Hair Spray agrees. "I've got to get home early to shower and change for tonight's Supervillian Awards Banquet."

"That's right, I'd almost forgotten," Burping Boy says. "The Awards are tonight."

Finally, I have an idea and type: "Okay guys, let's get back to the story."

But Burping Boy ignores me and asks Hair Spray, **"Aren't you up for best support-ing villain?"**

"That's right."

"Congratulations."

"Thanks."

"Guys—"

"What are you going to wear?"

"I thought maybe my black turtle-neck and—"

"Guys, that ground is really coming up fast!"

"—white tuxedo."

"That's a great choice."

"You don't think it makes me look fat?"

"No way."

"GUYS!"

"You sure?"

"You want to talk fat. Did you see Catwoman at last year's awards?"

"GUYS! WE'VE GOT TO HURRY. BURPER BOY IS JUST ABOUT TO HIT THE—"

K-SPLAT

"What was that?" Hair Spray Dude

demands. "Where's Burping Boy? What happened?"

I close my eyes, not believing my own imagination.

Hair Spray Dude continues shouting. "What happened to Burping Boy? What happened to Burping Boy?"

Reluctantly, I raise my fingers to the keyboard and type:

"Looks like you'll be getting home a lot earlier than you thought."

Talk about feeling lousy. I'd never killed off my characters so early in a story. Come to think of it, I'd never killed off any of my characters in any story. But before I could figure out how to bring him back, the phone

RING

rang.

Or is it

RANG

ringed?

(Never could get the hang of those past-tense verbs.)

I glanced at the clock. It was seven in the morning. Who would be calling now? Who would be so inconsiderate to bother me now when I needed all the rest I could get to recover?

I picked up the phone and gave the obvious answer, "Look, Wall Street, whatever it is you're planning, I'm not interested."

But, to my surprise, it wasn't Wall Street. It was . . .

"Mr. McDoogle, I require your assistance immediately!" In the background I heard all sorts of

*clink-clank-clunk*ing
and
*clunk-clank-clink*ing.

"Junior," I said, "what's wrong?"

"It is Tina. I accidentally struck her with the G.O.O.F. beam. She has broken out of her cage and seems to be growing larger by the

clink-clank-clunk

second."

"What's that got to do with me?" I asked.

"You are the only one who can—

clunk-clank-clink

reason with her. Hurry, she is approaching!"

"But—"

"I'll pay you enough to purchase the entire vase for your mother!"

"But, but—"

"Hurry!"

"But, but, but—"

"Please cease the motorboat imitation. She is now picking me up from the ground and—"

Suddenly, the phone went dead.

"Hello!" I shouted. "Hello, Junior? Junior, can you hear me?!"

I wasn't sure what to do. Call the police?

Maybe.

Tell Mom?

Maybe.

But he had promised to pay for the entire vase. And if all I had to do was sneak out and get Tina to relax by starting to giggle . . .

In a burst of nonintelligence I made up my mind. I leaped from the bed and

"Augh!"

K-thud

fell over that pile of kid videos. After regaining consciousness, I got dressed in the dark, slipped on my shoes, and

"Augh!"
K-thud.

After switching my shoes to the correct feet, I took off, doing my usual falling down the

k-bounce, k-bounce, k-bounce

falling down the stairs. I raced to the door, threw it open into

K-Bang
"OW!"

my face, and ran outside. Dawn was just breaking. In less than an hour I'd be done. In less than an hour I'd calm Tina by making her giggle, and then get all the money for the vase. In less than an hour my dream plan would finally become a reality.

Either that, or a nightmare . . .

Chapter 9

An Itsy-Bitsy ... MONSTER!

I arrived at Junior's lab in record time.

The good news was, Tina had grown to the size of a small car. (If you don't think that's good news, just keep reading.)

The bad news was, she was holding Junior Whiz Kid in her mouth, obviously considering him for breakfast.

"Hello, Mr. McDoogle," Junior said. He wore a raincoat and tried to sound calm so he wouldn't scare the hairy-legged critter. "How very nice of you to join us."

Trying to sound equally as calm, I quietly observed: "SHE'S GONNA EAT YOU ALIVE!!"

Unfortunately, this did little to relax Tina, who already seemed a bit on the tense side. (I guess growing to the size of a Volkswagen Beetle can be stressful even to tarantulas.) At the sound of my scream, she immediately rose up on her hind legs and started clawing the air.

"Excuse me," Junior called from high over my head. "I don't believe that is quite the response we are looking for. Might I suggest another approach?"

"WHAT?!" I cried.

"Slip on that leather flight helmet and those flight goggles there on the table. Then stand nice and close so she can smell you and recognize your scent."

I understood the smelling part, but not the leather helmet and those goggles.

"Spiders have venom, which is basically poison. Since the tests, Tina's venom is especially toxic," he explained. "If any were to drop into your eyes, you would go blind. If any were to drop onto your hair, you would go bald. That is why I managed to slip on this raincoat just before she got me."

Call me a chicken, but standing under a tarantula dripping with poison was not my idea of a good time—particularly with my rare medical condition, something called, "I'm Afraid to Die!"

But the little guy was definitely on his way to becoming spider food. So I grabbed the helmet and goggles, slipped them on, and carefully inched my way closer. "Nice Tina, Tina, Tina. Good girl, yes, you are."

She gave no response, well, except for rearing higher.

"What's wrong?" I shouted.

"Your scent appears to be insufficient."

"I'm stinking the best I can."

"With her larger size, she needs a larger scent."

"What else can we do?!"

"The G.O.O.F.!" Junior shouted. "Proceed to the G.O.O.F.!"

I slipped past Tina and raced over to the machine. "Now what?"

"Procure the G.O.O.F. helmet."

I jumped up on the chair and grabbed the helmet hanging from the electrical cable. "Now what?"

"Observe the knob on the right side of the helmet!"

"The one labeled '*SHRINK / ENLARGE*'?"

"Correct. Adjust the knob to *SHRINK*. Then start the machine, and direct the beam toward Tina."

I did everything he said and pointed the helmet at Tina.

So far, so good.

Immediately, the rays started to shoot

kuuuzch-kuuuzch-kuuuzch

at her.

So far-er, so good-er.

Unfortunately, that was as far-er and good-er as it got. Wanting to avoid hitting Junior with the beam (he was shrimpy enough already), I tried to adjust its aim by stepping around a little on the chair.

"Do not move!" Junior shouted. "Your position is quite adequate!"

But, being the perfectionist I am, I continued stepping back and forth.

The only problem was, my "back and forth" was a little bigger than the chair's "back and forth."

Translation: I accidentally stepped

"AUGH!"

off the chair and did my usual nosedive onto the

K-rack

floor.

But wait a minute. As any experienced *My Life As* . . . reader knows, the *K-rack* should have been *K-thud* (the sound my body always makes when hitting hard surfaces). A *K-rack* meant something else had hit the floor, instead of me. Something else like, oh, I don't know, maybe a very expensive (and now somewhat broken) G.O.O.F. helmet?

"A VERY EXPENSIVE G.O.O.F. HELMET?!"

(Sorry, I'm doing it again.)

I leaped to my feet and gave the helmet a quick once-over. Fortunately, I saw nothing wrong and resumed pointing it at

kuuuzch-kuuuzch-kuuuzch

Tina.

Unfortunately, I should have given it a twice-over because, instead of getting smaller, Tina was getting bigger—

"What is happening?!" Junior cried.

—and bigger—

kuuuzch-kuuuzch-kuuuzch

"I don't know!" I shouted.

—and bigger—

kuuuzch-kuuuzch-kuuuzch

"The controls, what have you done to the controls?!"

"Nothing," I shouted. Then, glancing at the helmet, I saw it. My crash-and-burn routine had busted off one tiny little knob.

Unfortunately, that one tiny little knob just happened to be the one labeled *"SHRINK/ENLARGE"*!

Unfortunatelier, when it broke off, it also jammed from the *"SHRINK"* setting to the *"ENLARGE"* setting. Other than that,

kuuuzch-kuuuzch-kuuuzch

everything was fine and dandy. Well, except for the part about Tina growing so quickly she immediately

*K-rash*ed

through the laboratory ceiling. Of course, this freaked her out (not to mention Junior, who was still in her grip)—so, as any typical rampaging monster would do, she broke down the wall and charged into the alley.

Ah, yes, the alley.

But instead of chasing a doggie-size snail, our latest pet was a tarantula the size of a small house, complete with two-car garage, one and a half baths, and central air. (All right, I exaggerated about the central air, but now do you see why the Volkswagen version of Tina had been good news?)

She scurried down the alley, squeezing her giant body between the walls of the buildings. And, since Junior Whiz Kid had transformed her soft skin into steel, the only thing that gave when she squeezed against the walls was

RIP-P-P
crumble, crumble, crumble

the walls.

No problem. Well, except for those people who had apartments next to the alley. But why should they complain? With their walls missing they were getting much better views and fresher air.

Meanwhile, Junior was going crazy, screaming his lungs out. "Would you be so kind as to assist me? Would you be so kind as to assist me?" (Obviously, his version of going crazy is a little different from mine.)

But neither of us had to worry. Tina used one leg to pull Junior from her jaws and set him atop her head. She wasn't interested in any human meals just yet. Right now she seemed more in the mood for appetizers—like the little flock of pigeons that was fluttering overhead. The little flock of pigeons that

snatch, snatch
CHOMP, CHOMP

HAD been fluttering overhead. Now they were
fluttering somewhere in her digestive system—
feathers and all. Which would explain her sud-
den case of

*hic-hic-hiccup*s

and the occasional

gag, choke
*cough, cough*ing

up of feathers.
   Now, the only thing worse than a giant, hiccuping tarantula coughing up feathers as it
scurries down an alley is a giant, hiccuping
tarantula coughing up feathers as it scurries
down an alley and out onto Main Street . . .
right into the middle of rush-hour

HONK, HONK
SQUEAL, SQUEAL
K-Rash, K-Rash

traffic.

Talk about a grand entrance. And, of course, everybody had something to say, like:

"WE'RE BEING INVADED!"
"OUR CITY IS BEING DESTROYED!"
"ARE WE IN ANOTHER McDOOGLE BOOK?"

Of course, I did my part, chasing Tina through the traffic, doing my best to dodge rolling hubcaps, flying glass, and an out-of-control bus.
"OUT-OF-CONTROL BUS?!"
(Sorry.)
The good news was, the bus

SCREECH

missed me. The bad news was, it didn't miss the courthouse lawn or the statue of our town's founder, Beauregard Bumbleburger.

K-BLAMB!
shatter, shatter, shatter

Talk about broken up. The guy was all over the place.
But Tina didn't stop.
During her pigeon feast, Junior had clung to the top of her head. I'm sure the view was much

better up there, but the fall (about fifty feet) was to die for (literally). So he hung on for dear life, still singing that same worn-out song, "Would you be so kind as to assist me?! Would you be so kind as to assist me?!"

Don't get me wrong, it was a catchy melody. I was just getting tired of the lyrics.

Apparently, so were the police. With lights flashing, they raced up, leaped out of their cars, and pulled out their guns.

"Don't shoot!" I cried. "Don't shoot!"

But I was too late.

K-pling! K-plang! K-zing!

That, of course, is the sound bullets make when bouncing off a giant tarantula whose skin has been turned to steel! Yes sir, things were looking worse and worse in a badder and badder sort of way.

Chapter 10

Wrapping Up

Tina continued doing her Godzilla impression through my little town. All this with plenty of

*Hic-hic-hiccup*ing,
*cough-cough-cough*ing
and
*hee-hee-hee*ing.

Wait a minute, was that a giggle? I looked up and shouted to Junior, "Did you hear that?"

"Yes!" he cried. "I believe it is Tina!"

"But how? Why?" And then I spotted it. She had just stepped on one of the pigeon tail feathers she'd coughed up. "A feather!" I shouted. "It tickled the bottom of her foot!"

"Yes," he cried. "I was unable to treat the bottom of her feet with the steel formula. They are the only part of her body still sensitive to touch!"

My mind went into overtime. "So maybe we could get her to laugh by tickling her feet. . . ."

Junior saw where I was going. "And perhaps she would roll onto her back as she did in the lab!"

"Yes!" I shouted. "That's our solution!"

"Except for one minor detail."

"What's that?"

"Who is crazy enough to try to tickle her feet?"

I looked around. Not the police. They were too busy

K-pling! K-plang! K-zing!-ing.

Not the crowd. They were too busy shouting:

"OUR TOWN IS BEING DESTROYED!"

There was no one to help. No one to step up to the plate and take responsibility to save our town.

Well, almost no one . . .

Because there, in the midst of all the chaos, it hit me . . . all my problems, from my giant ears, to the falling snail, to terrorizing the town . . . they'd all happened for one reason and one reason only: I hadn't been responsible enough to tell Mom the truth about the vase.

And Tina's condition? Wasn't I just as responsible (at least partially) for what was going on with her?

And if that was the case, then maybe, just maybe, the time had finally come. Maybe it was time for *me* to step up to the plate. Maybe it was time for *me* to quit dodging the truth and finally take *responsibility*.

Unfortunately, it was also time to see two army helicopters and a giant tank coming up over the horizon. Now, you didn't have to be a genius to know they were about to blast us to smithereens. No problem for me. All I had to do was turn tail and run. A perfect plan, except . . .

"Would you be so kind as to assist me?!"
"Would you be so kind as to assist me?!"

Junior was still atop Tina's back, crying for help. And if I didn't do something, he and Tina would both become the army's latest bull's-eye in target practice! No, I couldn't let that happen. Not and be . . . oh, no, there's that word again . . . *responsible*.

But I knew what I had to do. So, with a deep breath, and a prayer that God was taking notes, I rushed toward Tina. With a surge of courage, I grabbed the fallen tail feather and raced in

front of her to block her path. With a surge of
stupidity, I held out the feather like a cross in
some sort of vampire movie.

But apparently, Tina wasn't much of a film
buff. Instead of being afraid, she swooped down,
grabbed me between her jaws, and

"AUGH!"

threw me on top of her back beside Junior.

"Welcome!" Junior cried. "Do you have fur-
ther insight as to our next course of action?"

I tell you, the kid's vocabulary was starting
to bug me. But not as much as the helicopters
with their pesky

Whop Whop Whop Whop

and that tank with its even peskier artillery
that began

K-BLAMB! K-BLAM! K-BLAM!

firing at us!

Terrified by the explosions, Tina again
reared up on her hind legs. This allowed me to
utilize my incredible gift of clumsiness by accidentally rolling off her back. Luckily, I avoided

becoming road kill by grabbing hold of one of her legs. Unluckily, I grabbed hold of it upside down.

The explosions kept getting

K-BLAMB! K-BLAM! K-BLAM!

closer.

Tina panicked and started to run. No problem, except every step she to-oo-ok shook me like the belly of a fat ma-a-an using a jackhamm-er-er-er in the middle of an earthqua-a-ake.

So there I was, becoming the world's first human milk shake, when I heard Junior's irritating little voice shout, "Mr. McDoogle! Mr. McDoogle!"

"Wha-a-at?" I yelled.

"You still have possession of the feather!"

"So-o-o?"

"So reach down and tickle her foot with it!"

"A-re-re you nu-u-uts?!"

K-BLAMB! K-BLAM! K-BLAM!

"It appears to be our only solution!!"

With nothing else better to do, I figured I'd give it a shot. I stretched the feather toward Tina's foot. It didn't quite reach, so I climbed down even lower, which made my ride even bu-u-umpier. At last I could reach her toe with the feather. I started moving the tip back and forth. And, sure enough, she started

"Tee-hee-hee"-ing . . .

then

"Ho-ho-ho"-ing . . .

and, as she laughed, she began to slow.
"Keep it up, Mr. McDoogle! Keep it up!"
I did. And so did she . . . louder and

"Har-har-har . . ."

harder, until she couldn't take any more and—
"LOOK OUT! SHE'S ROLLING!"
Junior and I leaped off just as she flipped onto her back. Then, I quickly moved in to continue my attack as she kept right on

"Hee-hee, ho-ho, har-har!"-ing.

Spotting what had happened, the helicopters quickly swooped down and landed. Thankfully, the tank quit firing. And soon, both the army and the police were racing toward us. They brought in a veterinarian to give Tina a shot to knock her out. Actually, lots of shots . . . until she finally drifted off into tarantula tranquilizer land.

Meanwhile, all of those guys from the TV news closed in around me, demanding to know what it felt like to be a hero. I would have been happy to tell them, but I didn't have a clue. It was just me doing the same ol' same ol'! Just me going through another insane and absurd McDoogle mishap.

With Junior's careful instructions, they started building a crate to cart Tina back to his lab where he would repair the G.O.O.F. and shrink her back to normal size.

Yes sir, everything was getting back to normal—a wonderful storybook ending where everybody would live happily ever after.

Well, almost everybody . . .

"Wally?"

I turned to see Mom and Dad making their way through the crowd. I could tell by the tone of Dad's voice that he wasn't happy. But at least he didn't use my full name. Whenever that happens, I'm really in trouble.

"Wallace Ulysses McDoogle, you've got some explaining to do!"

Okay, now I'm in trouble.

I opened my mouth. I wanted to make up an excuse, but nothing came. I guess I knew it was time. It was time to tell the whole truth and nothing but the truth. And it was time to take . . . here's that word again . . . *responsibility* for my actions. Granted, it wasn't one of my favorite words, but it looked like it was definitely becoming one of the most important ones.

When we last left Burping Boy he'd become just so much smudge on the highway of life. Covered in hundreds of pounds of BBs, he'd fallen faster than a kid's smile when he learns he has to go to summer school. But, of course, it isn't the falling that hurts, but the

K-SPLAT-ting.

Still, with all those BBs attached, there's one other sound effect I forgot to mention. Since BBs tend to bounce, Burping Boy also tends to

K-Bounce.

"All right!" the hero shouts. "I knew you'd think of a way to save me!"

"Thanks," I type. "Now let's get on with the story."

"Cool."

In fact, he bounces so hard and high that soon he is shooting right back toward the helicopter—

"Oh, that's good! Real goo—"

"Please."

"Sorry."

He shoots right back toward Hair Spray Dude's helicopter. And with a few midcourse

burpa-burpa-burpas

he is able to fly through the open door and land on top of Hair Spray Dude!

"Hey!" Our villian shouts. "How did you get back up here?"

But this is no time to explain the author's great genius. Instead, it is time for the obligatory (there's an impressive word for your English

teacher) fight to the finish. That's
right, soon they are punching and
wrestling one another, rolling back
and forth, and forth and back. Yes
sir, it's a battle to the end (or at
least until one of them sprains a
pinky), when suddenly—

K-Bump

"What's *AH-CHOO!* that?" Hair Spray
Dude cries.

K-Bump, K-Bump

Looking out the doorway, Burping
Boy cries, "It's the dust bunny. He's
grown so big he's knocking into the
helicopter."
"*AH-CHOO!*" Hair Spray Dude shouts.
"What?" our hero yells.
"*AH-CHOO! AH-CHOO!*"
"Don't tell me you're allergic to
dust?"
"*AH-CHOO! AH-CHOO! AH-CHOO!*"
"You can't be creating dust bun-
nies to take over the world if you're
allergic to their dust!"

"You're right," Hair Spray Dude says, suddenly seeing the flaw in his plan—while trying to *sniff-sniff* back a stream flowing like the Amazon from his nose. "What shall I, *snort-snort*, do?"

"Well, first you have to find a tissue for that nose."

"All I got is, *sniff-sniff*, my shirt."

"That's disgusting, but if that's all you got..."

"Okay, hang on. *HOOOOONK!*"

Our hero swallows back a wave of revulsion, then continues. "Next, you have to be truthful and take responsibility for your actions."

"Truth and responsibility? Are you, *AH-CHOO*, sure?"

Wiping the spray from his face, our hero nods. "Absolutely. Just take a look at this new *My Life As . . .* book." With one swift move our hero whips out Book #22 and opens it. "You see right here, on page 3, where Wally falls down the stairs and breaks his mom's vase?"

"Yeah, *sniff-sniff*."

"And then, over here on page 4, where he tries to cover it up?"

"Not real smart, *snort-snort*, is he?"

"You can say that again. And check this out here: where he tries all those moneymaking schemes to buy another vase so his mom doesn't find out."

"Man, this guy's really, *sniff-snort*, clueless, isn't he?"

"All right," I type. "I think we get the point!"

But they do not hear, as they continue reviewing my latest adventure...as the dust bunny continues

K-Bump, K-Bumping

into the helicopter, and as Hair Spray Dude continues

"AH-CHOO! AH-CHOO!"-ing.

Fortunately, it doesn't last forever. As Hair Spray Dude keeps reading, he begins to realize the need to always tell the truth and take responsibility for his actions. Soon, the two of

them are planning a way to save the
world through a massive dust-sweeping
campaign——something involving super-
brooms. But the details aren't important. What's important is that Hair
Spray Dude has learned the need to
always tell the truth and take responsibility for his actions!

And so, as the two fly off into
the sunset,

(begin sappy credit music here)

we can rest assured, knowing that the
world will be a safer, saner, and——
"AH-CHOO!"——slightly less damp place
for each of us to live. All because
someone has learned a very important
lesson about...responsibility.

"Cool ending," Burping Boy says.

"Thanks," I type. "I couldn't have done it
without you."

"And we couldn't have done it
without, *sniff,* you," Hair Spray Dude
says. "Well, at least not without all
those incredibly ignorant mistakes
you made these last couple of weeks."

"Don't you have an awards banquet to attend?"

"Oh, yeah, *snort,* that's right."
With that, Hair Spray Dude turns and
starts to exit the story. "It was
fun," he calls. "Wish me luck!"

"Good luck!" I type.

"See ya!" Burping Boy shouts.

"*AH-CHOO!*" Hair Spray Dude cries
as he finally disappears from the
page.

I sat looking at the screen a moment. It
wasn't a bad story, but now what? I suppose I
could go downtown and attend the parade
everyone was throwing in my honor. The parade
that the rest of the town, even Tina, was cele-
brating at this very moment.

But it's hard attending a parade in your
honor when you've been grounded for life.

Yes, that was my folks' discipline (though I
suspect they'll go easy on me in a decade or
two). Still, their punishment was nothing compared to what I'd been through with my own
lying and dodging of responsibility. Actually, I
figured I got off pretty easy. And, if just sitting
at home with Mom and Dad for the afternoon
was what I had to do, then that was fine
with—

Ding-Dong.

Who could that be? I got up and headed for the door. Wasn't everyone at the parade? I reached the door, opened it, and saw—

"Hello, *giggle-giggle,* Wallace."

"Megan??" My voice went up ten octaves. "What are you doing here?"

"I heard about your having to stay home and figured, *snap-snap,* you might want some company. So I came over," she said, then snapped her gum again.

"Oh," I swallowed hard, "you didn't have to do that."

"Oh, but I wanted to," she said, batting her eyes.

I stood frozen, unsure what to do.

"So, *pop-pop*, can I come in?"

"Uh. . . ." I searched for an excuse, but nothing came to mind.

"I won't be a bother," she said, stepping past me and heading toward a chair.

I followed. "So, uh . . . what do you want to do?" I asked.

"I don't know."

"Oh," I said. "So, uh . . . what do you like to do?"

"I don't know."

"Oh," I said. (As far as conversations go, this one wasn't.)

She continued to stare. I continued to fidget.

"Well, you must like doing something?" I asked.

"I like to read."

"No kidding?" I asked, brightening a little.

"Yes. Especially superhero stories."

"No kidding?" I repeated, my voice kinda cracking in excitement as I glanced over at Ol' Betsy.

"Yes, but there aren't that many superhero stories around."

"Oh, really," I said. I walked over and snapped on Ol' Betsy. "I bet we might be able to find one or two you'd be interested in." (Actually, at last count I had 3,542—enough to keep her happy for hours.) And me? Well, finding somebody who actually liked reading what I wrote . . . well, maybe hanging with Megan Melkner wouldn't be so bad after all.

"Really?" She giggled. "That would, *snap-snap, pop-pop*, be like (sigh-sigh, bat-bat) so cool."

"Yeah," I said, passing Ol' Betsy over to her. "One can only hope (twitch, twitch), one can only (twitch, twitch) hope. . . ."

You'll want to read them all.

THE INCREDIBLE WORLDS OF WALLY McDOOGLE

#18—My Life As a Beat-Up Basketball Backboard

Ricko Slicko's Advertising Agency claims that they can turn the dorki-est human in the world into the most popular. And who better to prove this than our boy blunder, Wally McDoogle! Soon he has his own TV series and fans wearing glasses just like his. But when he tries to be a star athlete for his school basketball team, Wally finally learns that being popular isn't all it's cut out to be. (ISBN 0-8499-4027-3)

#19—My Life As a Cowboy Cowpie

Once again our part-time hero and full-time walking disaster area finds himself smack-dab in another misadventure. This time it's full of dude-ranch disasters, bungling broncobusters, and the world's biggest cow—well, let's just say it's not a pretty picture (or a pleas-ant-smelling one). Through it all, Wally learns the dangers of seeking revenge. (ISBN 0-8499-5990-X)

#20—My Life As Invisible Intestines

When Wally becomes invisible, he can do whatever he wants, like humiliating bullies, or helping the local football team win. But the fun is short-lived when everyone from a crazy ghostbuster to the *59 1/2 Minutes* TV show to the neighbor's new dog begin pursuing him. Soon Wally is stumbling through another incredi-ble disaster . . . until he finally learns that cheating and taking shortcuts in life are not all they're cracked up to be and that honesty really is the best policy. (ISBN 0-8499-5991-8)

#21—My Life As a Skysurfing Skateboarder

Our boy blunder finds himself participating in the Skateboard Championship of the Universe. (It would be "of the World" except for the one kid who claims to be from Jupiter—a likely story, in spite of his two heads and seven arms.) Amid the incredible chaotic chaos by incurably corrupt competitors (say that five times fast), Wally learns there is more to life than winning. (ISBN 0-8499-5592-6)

MEET WALLY McDOOGLE'S COUSIN

Trouble (and we're talking BIG trouble) runs in Wally's family. Follow his younger cousin Secret Agent Bernie Dingledorf and his trusty dog, Splat, as they try to save the world from the most amazing and hilarious events.

SECRET AGENT DINGLEDORF
... and his trusty dog, SPLAT °᠂°

BY BILL MYERS

1—*The Case of the Giggling Geeks*

The world's smartest people can't stop laughing. Is this the work of the crazy criminal Dr. Chuckles? Only Secret Agent Dingledorf (the country's greatest agent, even if he is only ten years old) can find out. Together, with supercool inventions (that always backfire), major mix-ups (that become major mishaps), and the help of Splat the Wonder-dud, er, Wonder-dog, our hero winds up saving the day . . . while discovering the importance of respecting and loving others.
(ISBN: 1-4003-0094-0)

2—*The Case of the Chewable Worms*

The earth is being invaded by worms! They're everywhere . . . crawling on kids' toothbrushes, squirming in their sandwiches, making guest appearances in Mom's spaghetti dinner. And, worst of all, people find them . . . tasty! But is it really

an invasion or the work of B.A.D.D. (Bungling Agents Dedicated to Destruction)? Only Secret Agent Dingledorf and his trusty dog, Splat, can find out and save the day . . . while also realizing the importance of doing good and helping others.
(ISBN: 1-4003-0095-9)

3—*The Case of the Flying Toenails*

It started out with just one little lie. But now, everybody is coming down with the dreaded disease—Priscilla, parents, even Super-dud, er, Super-dog, Splat. They go to bed perfectly normal one night, then wake up the next morning with jet-powered toenails! Who knows the truth behind this awful sickness? Who can stop it? Only Secret Agent Dingledorf and his not-so-trusty (at least in this book) sidekick Splat can find the cure and save the day . . . while discovering how important it is to be honest and always tell the truth.
(ISBN: 1-4003-0096-7)

4—*The Case of the Drooling Dinosaurs*

What's going on? Why are there dinosaurs slobbering all over the city? Is this the work of Dr. Rebellion, the man who hates following the rules? Only Secret Agent Dingledorf and his trusty dog, Splat, can find the answer. Only they can save the day while also learning the importance of obeying those in charge. This funny, zany story is an adventure about following rules— and the chaos that happens when we don't!
(ISBN: 1-4003-0177-7)

And look for upcoming releases!